Weekly Reader Books presents

The Sick Story

story by Linda Hirsch
pictures by John Wallner

HASTINGS HOUSE · PUBLISHERS
New York, 10016

For my very own "Maaaa" and Dad

Miranda had the sniffles.

It began as an itch in her nose and a few sneezes. People said, "Gesundheit!" but not much else.

Then her nose got stuffy. She'd close one nostril and blow out through the other trying to get air. Miranda certainly felt awful and she said so.

"Oh boy, do I feel awful."

Her mother kissed her forehead and said she had a slight fever. "It's just a cold." She sent her to bed with an aspirin and a glass of orange juice. Miranda settled under the covers and picked up a comic book.

She tried to read but she really couldn't concentrate. She touched her forehead. It did feel a little warm. A few seconds later she checked it again. "I'm not any warmer," she reassured herself.

Her father came in and set up a vaporizer.

"Daddy, don't put it too close to me. I can't breathe with all that steam blowing in my face." Her father sighed and moved it away from the bed.

"It won't help anyway," said Miranda, drawing the covers up under her chin. "When you're sick, you're sick."

Miranda believed there was only *one* way to get over a cold. No school for at least two days and the *best* of care.

"Maaaaaa," she yelled. "I need a tissue." Her mother came in with tissues.

"Maaaaaa!" called Miranda ten minutes later. Her mother came in.

"These tissues scratch my nose. I need a hanky." Her mother returned with a hanky.

"I'll have some toast now, if you please," said Miranda.

"And don't burn it," she added.

Her mother brought her toast with butter and jam on a little tray with flowers painted on it. Miranda was developing quite an appetite, not to mention a thirst.

"Maaaaaa!" Miranda's voice cut through the house. "Oh, Maaaaaaaaa!" There was no answer. Now where could she be?

Her mother came in with her arms full of laundry. "Is anything the matter?" she asked calmly.

"I'm thirsty. Could I have some tea?"

"Do you think you can wait until I put the laundry in?"

"I guess so," said Miranda. After what seemed like a rather long time to keep a sick person waiting, Miranda's mother returned with a cup of tea. Miranda sipped at it.

"It's really very hot," she complained.

"It's better for you when it's hot," said her mother. Miranda looked doubtful.

"There's not enough sugar in it. Could you bring some more, please?"

Room service continued for the rest of that day. Miranda's

mother fluffed her pillow, brought her the latest movie maga-
zines and administered two teaspoons of cough medicine every
four hours.

"How lucky my mother is to have me to take care of,"
thought Miranda. "It certainly keeps her occupied."

Her father dropped by to see how Miranda was feeling.
"Not very well, I'm afraid," said Miranda. "Being sick is very
tiring."

"I know," said her father, looking at her in a very tired
way.

Miranda woke up at seven o'clock the next morning. She noticed one thing right away. She could breathe.

Maybe she was better, maybe even well enough to go to school. The thought made her sleepy, and a little achy, too.

"Kids are germy," said Miranda. "You never know what

you might catch from them. Maybe even strep throat. Uggh! The risks aren't worth it!"

Miranda stayed home.

She lay in bed, watching the TV her father brought into her room. She loved reruns of old shows. Game shows were okay, too.

Perching herself on the edge of the bed, Miranda listened very closely.

"I'm going to ask you a question," said the announcer to one of the players. "As soon as you know the answer, push your buzzer. What famous American wrote *Poor Richard's Almanac?*"

"Benjamin Franklin! Benjamin Franklin!" Miranda was jumping up and down. "I know it! I know it!"

The player looked at the announcer. Her face was blank.

"Push the buzzer, dummy!" shrieked Miranda. "It's Benjamin Franklin!"

"Oh, I'm not really sure," said the woman sadly.

"It's Benjamin Franklin! Benjamin Franklin!" Miranda yelled at her.

"I'm sorry, Betty. Your time is up. The correct answer is Benjamin Franklin." The audience gave a loud sigh.

"I knew it! I knew it!" Miranda stamped her foot.

"Tune in tomorrow when our players compete for a trip to Hawaii!"

"Hawaii?" echoed Miranda. "I bet I could win a trip to Hawaii."

Suddenly, strange music began to play. "And now, for the next thirty minutes, *Love of Life.*"

What could that be? Miranda snuggled under the covers and began to watch. She was so absorbed that she didn't hear her mother come in.

"Here's lunch."

"Shhh!" hissed Miranda. A couple were having a fight. They were arguing about someone named Arlene. Her mother set down a tray. "Don't shhh me!"

Eyes fixed on the TV, Miranda took a spoonful of chicken soup. Her hand slipped. "Oh no," she whispered. There were noodles on her new nightgown.

"That's it! No more TV."

"Ma! Leave it on *one* more minute! *Please!*"

"I said no. If you're so sick you don't need TV." With that her mother clicked off the set. Miranda made a face.

"Mothers certainly have weird ideas," she grumbled. Left alone, she finished her soup and grilled cheese sandwich, gulped her milk and bit the chocolate chips out of her cookies.

For the first time that day, Miranda felt bored. She looked around for something to do.

She picked up a wad of colored paper and her big box of crayons and began to draw.

"Oh, that's terrible! she said, crumpling up the first one.

Maybe I'm using too much blue." She tossed aside the second and third drawings, too.

"These are just not turning out right," she muttered. "It must be these crayons. They have no points."

The fifth drawing was more successful. "If that doesn't look like a tree, I don't know what does," said Miranda quite satisfied.

"Glad to see you're feeling better, Miranda." She looked up. There was her father standing in the doorway.

"Oh no I don't, Daddy," she said, dropping her crayon. "I've been trying to draw but it's no use. I just don't feel up to it."

Miranda climbed back into bed. "Colds are so hard to shake." Her father smiled and walked off and Miranda sat staring at the map on her wall.

At 3:30, her friend Rebecca stopped by with the homework. Miranda trudged into the living room. As soon as she
saw Rebecca, she felt her nose stuff up.

"How do you feel?" asked Rebecca.

"Not so good." Miranda lay down on the couch and propped two pillows behind her head. Rebecca sat next to her.

"You'd better not sit here, Rebecca. Sit over there," said Miranda, pointing across the room. "I'm contagious."

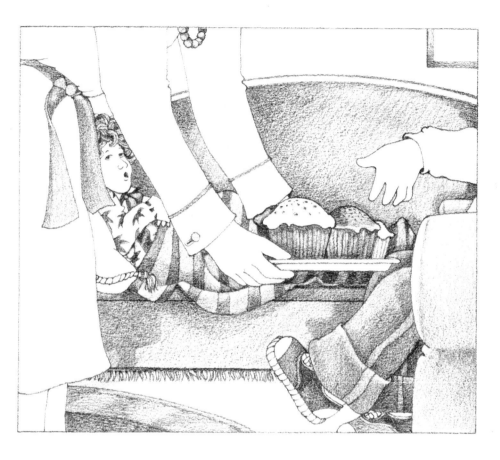

Miranda's mother brought in chocolate milk and cup-cakes. "These are my favorite morsels!" said Rebecca, picking up one with sprinkles.

"Morsels?" thought Miranda. "Where does she get those words?"

"As usual, there's too much science," sighed Rebecca, crumbs falling from her lips.

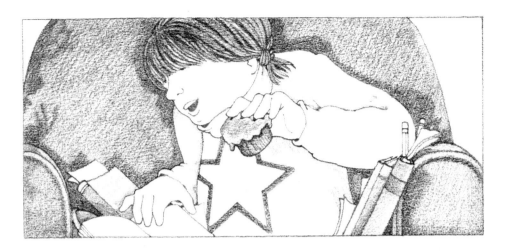

"How can she eat so much?" thought Miranda. "I can't eat a thing."

"Leila filled in all the answers during recess. Doesn't it make you sick, Miranda, the way she always finishes everything ahead of time? It makes me sick."

Rebecca began biting the icing off another cake. "There's math also. I could teach it to you but I really have to go home and rehearse my part in the play."

"What play?" coughed Miranda.

"The class play. We're doing *Alice in Wonderland.* Have you ever read it?"

"I also saw the movie," replied Miranda haughtily.

"I'm the Cheshire Cat," Rebecca continued. "I smile all the time. It'll probably hurt my mouth."

Miranda sat up. "Does everyone have a part?" she asked. "Well, Warren's the Mad Hatter. And Suzy is Alice. Everybody's something. Except nobody's the Queen of Hearts yet." Miranda looked interested.

"That's a very difficult part. It's too bad you're sick, Miranda. You're such a talented actress."

Miranda couldn't disagree.

"Why not try out tomorrow? Of course, getting better is more important."

Again, Miranda couldn't disagree, but she was having her doubts.

After Rebecca had gone, she walked slowly back to her room. Her talents were being wasted. Some stupid person was going to get a part that she was meant to play. She popped a cough drop into her mouth and bit all the way through it, cracking it in two. Then she thought for a long time.

"Well, I can't disappoint the class that way."

That night she refused room service and came in to dinner.

"I'm going back to school tomorrow," she announced.

"Feeling better?" asked her mother, looking not so surprised.

"Much," answered Miranda.

"Well, I'm not sure, Miranda. After all, you can't be too careful. You might get sick again."

"I feel great. I can go to school. Besides I want to be in the play."

"Oh, I see," said her father, smiling to her mother.

Miranda was getting embarrassed, but she was even more afraid they'd make her stay home.

"I really wasn't all that sick anyway. I mean—you know."

"Hmmm," said her mother. "I guess you're well enough to help with the dishes tonight."

"I guess so," sighed Miranda.

"Maybe clean up your room, too?"

"Yes, that too," said Miranda loudly blowing her nose. There was no sense in letting them think she was 200% well.

"How about your homework?" Was there no end?

"That too," said Miranda.

"Well, then I guess it would be all right for you to go back."

Miranda jumped up from the table, hugged her parents and ran to her room.

She sat down by the window, pleased with her victory. But strange thoughts began to creep into her head. Maybe she wouldn't be that good in the play. She'd been known to forget a line or two. Maybe she *was* taking chances going back to school so soon after her dreadful cold.

"Relapses are common," she thought. "If I don't watch it, I could need a doctor next time. Maybe even a penicillin shot!"

"Why did I make such a fuss about going back to school?" she berated herself.

School! The play was one thing. But homework, tests, compositions — they were quite another. No talking, going to the library, doing reports, standing in line.

Miranda looked in the mirror. Her eyes seemed watery. She was probably still sick. Couldn't her parents see? Why didn't her mother insist she stay home? What kind of parents were they anyway, letting her go back just because she said she felt better? Parents were supposed to be so smart!

But the play! Tomorrow was probably her last chance to be the Queen of Hearts. If she didn't show up she'd be out of the play forever.

"Oh, life isn't easy!" thought Miranda. Why couldn't she have both? Stay in bed *and* go back to school in time for the play. Didn't anybody care about sick children?

Miranda looked around her room. She went to the closet to choose her clothes for the next day. It would have to be something special, something she felt right in. Looking through the closet made her even more nervous.

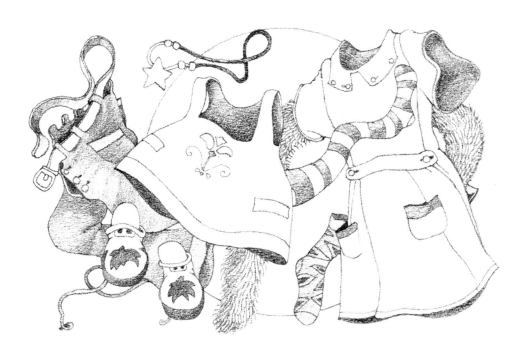

She glanced at her bed. It was full of crumpled tissues and hankies. There was her teacup.

"Oh dear," she thought, eyeing her comics. "What have I done? I want to stay home."

Miranda washed her face, brushed her teeth and put Vaseline on her red nose.

"It's not too late. I can still walk into the living room right now and tell them I'm sick. I look sick. I feel sick. They'll believe me." She headed for the door.

Then she stopped. "It's no use," she said. She was picturing herself wearing a long red dress with red hearts, reciting her lines. The audience would applaud. They'd love her.

"I'm going, that's it. The risks are worth it." Miranda got into bed, pulled the blankets up to her chin, gave a long sigh and one loud blow of her nose. Then she fell asleep.

When morning came, she put on her favorite red jumper over her blue and red sweater. She pulled on her beige knee socks with purple stars and her shiny red clogs. "I do look rather nice," she thought to herself.

She walked into the kitchen, nibbled on a piece of toast and swallowed some cough medicine just to be on the safe side. Then she kissed her mother good-bye.

Out on the street, Miranda saw other kids on their way to school. A bunch of them were standing on the corner waiting for the light to change. Miranda hesitated. Then she joined them.

And as she did, she smiled to herself.

"Bravo Miranda!"